BIBLELAND
Storybook

The STORY Of EASTER

Written by Alice Joyce Davidson
Illustrated by Victoria Marshall

Text copyright ©1988 by Alice Joyce Davidson
Art copyright ©1988 by The C.R. Gibson Company
Published by The C.R. Gibson Company
Norwalk, Connecticut 06856
Printed in the United States of America
All rights reserved
GB 311
ISBN 0-8378-1839-7

The C.R. Gibson Company, Norwalk, Connecticut 06856

A little girl named Alice
Was so happy it was Spring.
She loved to see the flowers
And to hear the robins sing.

Alice sat down in her garden
Underneath some budding trees;
Her favorite Bible storybook
Was propped up on her knees.

She chose to read of Easter
Which was just five days away.
And as she read, the airmail bird
Brought this note her way:

"Reading is the magic key
To take you where you want to be."

The Bible storybook she read
Became a giant screen.
She walked on through to Bibleland
And came upon this scene.

This early Sunday morning
Just as the dawn was breaking,
Three women walked up to a tomb;
Their hearts were sorely aching.

Their beloved teacher, Jesus,
Who was wonderful to know,
Was killed by those who feared Him
Just two short days ago.

They saw the stone that sealed His tomb
Had been rolled away.
Inside, the tomb was empty.
The women feared to stay.

One woman, Mary Magdelene,
Ran off to tell two others—
John and Peter, Jesus' friends
Whom He'd treated as dear brothers.

All three ran back to the tomb.
Peter, then John, too,
Found that the tomb was empty.
What Mary'd said was true!

Although the tomb was empty,
John and Peter found
Cloths which had wrapped Jesus
Lying on the ground.

Feeling scared and puzzled,
John and Peter left the tomb.
Mary stood outside and wept;
Her heart was filled with gloom.

She looked inside the half-lit tomb
And saw two angels near.
They asked, "Why are you weeping?"
She replied, "My Lord's not here."

A man who stood behind her
Asked why she wept still more?
Then gently He asked Mary
Whom she was looking for?

Mary didn't see the man.
The light was very dim.
She thought he was a gardener,
And so she said to him . . .

"If you know where they've taken Him,
Please, please do let me know.
Wherever they have taken Him,
That's where I want to go!"

The man just answered, "Mary."
All at once she knew His voice!
Mary knew the man was Jesus,
And she felt her heart rejoice.

Mary cried out, "Master!"
And quickly turned around.
Lovingly she kissed His feet
As she knelt upon the ground.

Jesus said to Mary
That she should go and tell
His loving friends and followers
That he was alive and well.

"I'm going to my God, my Father
Who is your God and Father, too.
And even though I'll be with Him,
I'll always be with you."

Mary ran and told His friends
That Jesus was not dead,
But they were much too doubtful
To believe anything she said.

His followers were frightened,
And so that very night
They secretly met inside a room
And locked the door real tight.

They feared the foes of Jesus
And felt they had to hide.
Then suddenly one noticed
Jesus standing by his side!

His friends thought Jesus was a ghost.
He sensed their frightened mood,
And then to prove He was alive,
Jesus asked for food.

When they saw Jesus eating,
They rejoiced for then they knew
That he was truly risen.
What Mary'd said was true!

Jesus said that soon He'd send
The Holy Spirit to them
To help them share the happy news
That Jesus lives again.

He said they all should preach
His teachings every day,
And they should baptize everyone
Who follows in His way.

The time had come for Alice
To leave that Bible scene.
She came back home by walking through
Her very special screen.

She took her book inside and thought,
"There are so many reasons
Why Easter's such a holy time
The happiest of seasons."

"On Easter morning Jesus rose
He was no longer dead.
And everything had happened
In just the way He'd said."

"His church was born on Easter
When He told His friends to share
The Good News of His teachings
With people everywhere."

Then Alice thought, "I'm glad to be
A friend of Jesus, too.
I'll spread His Word and feel Him near
Each day my whole life through."